MY VERY SPECIAL FRIEND

MY VERY SPECIAL FRIEND

LUCILLE E. HEIN
Illustrated by Joan Orfe

Judson Press, Valley Forge

MY VERY SPECIAL FRIEND

Library of Congress Cataloging in Publication Data

Hein, Lucille E
    My very special friend.

    SUMMARY: A five-year-old tells about a special visit with Great-Grandmother while Mother is in the hospital.
    [1. Grandmothers—Fiction. 2. Family—Fiction]
I. Title.
PZ7.H3677My   [E]   73-16790
ISBN 0-8170-0618-4

Printed in the U.S.A.

To my Mother
who is the Great Grandmother
of this story

My Very Special Friend

My mother is sick.
She is in the hospital—
   but not for long.
The doctor told me
   she would be home soon.

While Mother is in the hospital,
   my little brother is with friends.
Daddy is home alone.
And I—I am living with
       Grandmother
       and Grandfather
       and Great Grandmother.

I know Grandmother and Grandfather.
I often stay with them.

But I do not know Great Grandmother.
She is new to me.

Great Grandmother has white hair.
Her voice is soft.
She walks slowly.
She naps often,
    much more than I nap.

She is kind. She does not mind
    if I squeeze into her rocking chair.
She knows I am lonely . . .
    lonely for Mother, Daddy, and Brother.

1 2 3 4 5

6 7 8 9 10

11 12 13 14 15

16 17

Great Grandmother is very old.
  I am five.
  She is eighty-five!
  Great Grandmother says
    she is seventeen times as old as I.
  I cannot count to eighty-five.
  Not even to seventeen!

"Will I ever be eighty-five?" I asked.

Great Grandmother laughed and hugged me.
"Of course you will.
In our family we live long lives
  and we enjoy life."

$$\begin{array}{r} 17 \\ \times 5 \\ \hline 85 \end{array}$$

I miss my mother and daddy and brother.
But I have made Great Grandmother
   my very special friend while I am here.

We play games together. Easy games.

We take short walks
      around the house and garden,
      up and down the driveway,
      back and forth on our block.

We fill my wading pool from the hose.
We feed old bread to the birds and squirrels.
We watch a rabbit lunching on lettuce.

We tell one another secrets.
We teach one another how to do things.

When I came to stay here,
   Grandmother and Grandfather told me,
   "Great Grandmother is much older than you
   and not as strong as you.
You can help her in many ways."

"How?" I asked.

"Oh—in little ways.
We will not have to tell you.
You will see for yourself
   how you can help her."

I do see!

When we go in the car,
   I hold the door wide
   until Great Grandmother is all
      inside
   before I shut it.

When she sits on the patio in the sun,
 she asks me to run in for her sweater
 because she feels the wind on her back.

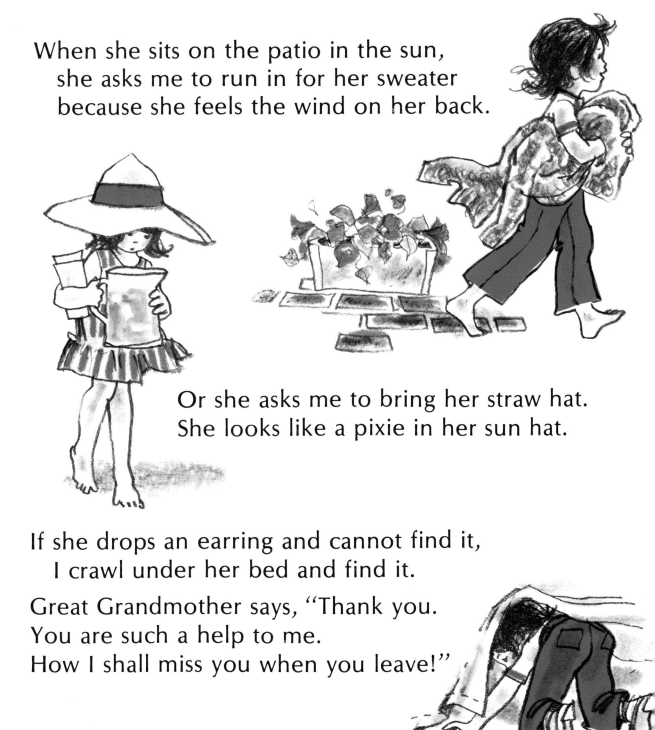

Or she asks me to bring her straw hat.
She looks like a pixie in her sun hat.

If she drops an earring and cannot find it,
 I crawl under her bed and find it.

Great Grandmother says, "Thank you.
You are such a help to me.
How I shall miss you when you leave!"

Sometimes Great Grandmother and I
   walk to a small park near our house,
      past a store and a few houses,
      around a corner,
      past two dogs who yip at us.

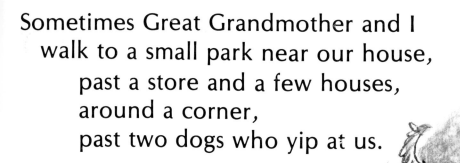

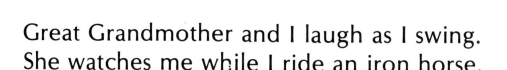

Great Grandmother and I laugh as I swing.
She watches me while I ride an iron horse.

When I see Great Grandmother is tired,
   I say, "Let's sit at a table and talk."

We sit at a table under a tree.
We play guessing games.
We look up through the leaves to the sky.
We listen to the birds sing.

When she is rested, we walk home.
I walk very slowly. I do not run or jump.
I might knock her over.
She is so tiny.

Once I asked her,
  "Why are you so small?"

She said,
  "You become smaller as you grow older.
Everything that was once so easy to do
  is hard to do when you are old.
Everything you once did so quickly
  must be done slowly when you are old."

One day Great Grandmother said,
"Let's plan a surprise for your mother
when she comes home from the hospital.
What surprise could you bring her?"

"Something to help her be well?" I asked.

"Yes. Something you learn to do yourself.
When you learn to do things yourself,
   you help your mother and father."

Great Grandmother thought about a surprise.

"I have it!" Great Grandmother called.

I was playing in another room
   but I heard her and ran to her.
"What will be my surprise?" I asked.

"You shall learn to tie your shoelaces!
That will help your mother.

"We will start now.
Take off your right shoe.
Stand beside me.
Watch me."

How Great Grandmother and I worked!
It was hard to learn to tie shoelaces.

But suddenly one day
everything was easy
   and I tied my shoelaces
myself!

I cannot wait
    for Mother to be home from the hospital.

Mother tried to teach me
    to tie my shoelaces.
I could not learn.
Maybe I was too little then.

Now I am bigger.
Now I shall go home
    and show Mother what I have learned.
Now I shall teach my little brother
    how to tie his shoelaces.
That will help Mother and Daddy.

Great Grandmother says
   when I learn to do something like
      tying my shoelaces,
      blowing my nose in a tissue,
      brushing my teeth carefully,
      printing my name,
   I will never forget how to do that thing.

Great Grandmother says
   that is why older people
   spend much time teaching younger people.

She says she likes to have me around
   so she can teach me things
   and so I can teach her things.

Great Grandmother has a cozy room.
It is full of things
   I like to look at and touch.

She lets me
     empty her drawers,
     look in her boxes,
     play with her jewelry,
     walk in her shoes.

I sit in her room and draw pictures.
She puts my pictures on her table
   and calls everyone in to see them.

She mends my clothes while I live here.
She likes to sew and teaches me to sew.
I use a thick, blunt needle
    and heavy string,
    and I sew on paper.
Great Grandmother says all boys and girls
    should know how to sew a little.

Great Grandmother has two footstools
    by her rocking chair in the living room.
One is for her feet.
One is for her magazines and newspapers.

She found a third footstool someplace.
And this is where I sit—
    right by her rocking chair.

We watch television together.
We play games.
We write letters to my mother.
Great Grandmother writes the words,
    and I draw pictures for the letters.

We cut pictures from magazines
    and tell stories about them.

When Great Grandmother reads to me,
    she lets me squeeze into her chair
    so I can see the pictures as she reads.

Sometimes she reads from her Bible.
She never tires of reading her Bible.
Her Bible is old and ragged and torn,
    but she does not want a new Bible.

"I've always had this Bible,
ever since I was ten years old."

Great Grandmother likes to go to church,
but she is too old to go to church often.
She grows tired sitting that long.
She does not like the crowds.

So she and I go to church on television.
Great Grandmother sings all the hymns
and repeats the prayers and Bible verses.
I know some of the hymns, too.
I am learning them in Sunday school.

Great Grandmother taught me to whistle.
She cannot whistle any longer.
She has too little breath.
But she can teach others how to whistle.

When I learned to whistle, she said,
    "What a surprise this will be for Mother.
Now you have two surprises to take home."

"Yes!" I shouted.
"I used to can't,
    but now I can!
Now I can whistle!
Now I can tie my shoelaces!"

I whistled so much
   that Great Grandmother
   and Grandmother and Grandfather
   held their hands over their ears.

"Stop!" Great Grandmother said.

Now I only whistle when I am outdoors.

One day Great Grandmother showed me
   how to choose a wide blade of grass,
   hold it between my thumbs,
   put it to my lips, and blow.
And it is a whistle.

And she taught me how to make a cold drink
   with instant mix and water and ice.

Great Grandmother knows so much.
I learn so much from her.
But she says she learns from me, too!

I wonder if Great Grandmother
    would like to learn to somersault.
I can somersault.

I asked her.

She laughed.
"I used to somersault—long ago—
    and stand on my head,
    and walk on my hands, too."

She knows how to do everything.
So how can she say she learns from me?

Sometimes we go to a store a block away.
I help her at the curbs.
She watches for cars.

At the store we buy something we need—
bread, milk, eggs.
Great Grandmother lets me pick a treat—
animal crackers,
popcorn,
ice cream on a stick,
candy bar.

She buys the same treat for herself.
She likes exactly what I like.

Great Grandmother talks about my family.
She shows me pictures.
She has boxes and boxes of pictures,
    people I do not know,
    people who lived long ago.

In my family
    there is Great Grandmother.
She is the oldest.

My grandmother is her child.
My mother is Grandmother's child.
And I am Mother's child.

It is hard for me to understand.
Great Grandmother says this is
    just a part of our family tree.

Everyone has a family, she says.
But some people do not know their family.
Some people do not love their family.
Some people run away from their family.

"In our family we love one another,"
  I told Great Grandmother.

"We certainly do," she said.
"And I love you so much."
Then she kissed me
  and I kissed her.

Great Grandmother
   and Grandmother and Grandfather
   go often to see my mother in the hospital.

One day Great Grandmother said,
"Your mother leaves the hospital today.
Tomorrow you will go home to her.
She sends you her love."

I cannot wait to see Mother.
   Wait till she hears me whistle!
   Wait till she sees me tie my shoelaces!
   Wait till she sees my drawings and sewing!

Will Mother know me?
Or will she think I am someone different?

"What present can you take your mother?"
Great Grandmother asked me.

"I have all my surprises," I said.

"Yes—but you need one special surprise."

She thought hard. "I know!" she said.
"You can write a poem to say to Mother."

And this is the poem I will say
    when Daddy takes me to Mother
    tomorrow . . .
        Every day
        you were away
        I thought of you
        and loved you.